MW01231554

BOSS' SECRET BABY

A BILLIONAIRE'S SECOND CHANCE ROMANCE

MICHELLE LOVE

HOT AND STEAMY ROMANCE

CONTENTS

Made in "The United States" by:

Michelle Love

© Copyright 2021

ISBN: 978-1-64808-755-4

❀ Created with Vellum

ABOUT THE AUTHOR

Mrs. Love writes about smart, sexy women and the hot alpha billionaires who love them. She has found her own happily ever after with her dream husband and adorable 6 and 2 year old kids. Currently, Michelle is hard at work on the next book in the series, and trying to stay off the Internet.

"Thank you for supporting an indie author. Anything you can do, whether it be writing a review, or even simply telling a fellow reader that you enjoyed this. Thanks

BLURB

He was supposed to be one of us. That's who I fell in love with, not the greedy bastard he became. How was I to know he was destined to be a part of my family...in more ways than one?

Javier Child was everything I'd ever wanted in a man: kind, sexy, and down to earth. No one would ever have known he was the boss's son if he didn't tell us.

Ever since that tryst at the Christmas party, I'd been wondering what it would be like to go all the way with him.

Whoever said *be careful what you wish for* knew exactly what they were talking about.

1

CHAPTER ONE

Aura

"Is this a fucking joke?"

I tensed at Steph's tone and turned to look at what she saw, her eyes poring over a memo on the break room bulletin board.

"What is it?" I asked lightly. "They're bringing meatloaf back?"

"No!" She snapped, giving me a contemptuous look. "It's our health insurance, Aura."

With a flip of a hand as if talking to me was a waste of her breath, she stormed out, leaving me staring after her. I'm not sure why she still caused a knot of tension in my stomach. After all, I'd been working with the miserable cow for two years. Her free use of expletives and surly attitude were hardly shocking but there was something about her...

She reminded me of my mother.

I steadied my breathing and turned to look at what she was reading and sighed heavily. For once, I agreed with Steph. It was bullshit.

The memo, written by someone in upper management who had probably spent all of two minutes dictating it to his secretary and probably even less time giving any thought to its repercussions.

Fellow employees of Child Motors, it began. *Commencing February 1ˢᵗ, the company will discontinue the practice of covering 80 percent of employee Apex Insurance premiums. Also, all medical, prescription, and dental benefits in the basic comprehensive insurance bundle will now be subject to a 50 percent copay, and mental health or physiotherapy services, including massage benefits, are no longer covered at this time.*

The above-listed benefits are still available at the Apex Gold premier insurance level. Please speak to your resident payroll administrator for the current rates of that premium plan.

Also, please note that employee life insurance benefits have been cancelled across the board due to company budget cuts.

Thank you for your cooperation in this matter.

MANAGEMENT

I stared and reread the memo for so long that my eyes got blurry.

This country is going to hell in a handbasket, I thought bitterly. *They just gouge us piece by piece until we're all right back to just scraping by.*

The insurance benefits were the reason I'd opted to work at the luxury car company in the first place. It certainly wasn't the twelve bucks an hour I was getting. My paycheck barely covered my most basic expenses.

Lucky for me, I was used to pinching my pennies. I hadn't had much of a choice during my childhood. My mom's gambling addiction had left me and my little brother Alex without food so many times, I had learned to squirrel money away for those days when she took off to Vegas on gambling binges.

"You've been standing there a long time."

The statement caused me to spin, partially because I was embarrassed at being caught doing nothing but mostly because I recognized the voice at my back even before his steely blue eyes locked with my green ones.

"I was just reading the memo," I sighed, reaching for the now-cold coffee I'd left on the counter by the coffee maker.

Javier shook his dark blonde head in disbelief.

"He's such a prick," he growled, shoving a pile of files onto the round table at the center of the room before snatching the memo off the board, crumpling it in his hands and shooting it into the wastebasket.

I was mildly impressed that he made the shot. I hadn't realized that Javvy played ball. Not that he didn't have the body for it; he was at least six foot three and muscled in precisely the right spots.

Even as I thought it, I found my eyes moving over his sculpted arms, a flash of heat burning through my body. The Christmas party hadn't been that long ago. I wonder if he still remembered our little tryst in the coatroom at the Carrington Arms. I've thought about it more than I should.

"You know, someone might have wanted to read that," I commented dryly, nodding toward the discarded paper, but I deliberately turned my dark mane of hair away, so he wouldn't read the blush on my face.

"It's overkill. Sadistic," Javvy snickered. "They already sent out an e-mail to everyone. Putting it up here is just adding insult to injury."

I admitted I was a bit touched by his annoyance. He had nothing to worry about. These changes weren't going to affect him in any way.

I shrugged and dumped the old coffee I had made into the sink, reaching for another mug in the rack.

"You want one?" I asked, and he nodded, exhaling in a huff of anger which I knew had nothing to do with me.

"Black, right?"

Javvy blinked and nodded, his head cocking to the side slightly.

"You remembered?"

My cheeks, which were finally returning to their normal color, flushed crimson again.

"It's not that hard to remember," I quipped even though I felt like kicking myself.

Could you show him that you have a ridiculous girl crush on him any more than you already have?

I got the sense that signal flares were springing from my eyes every time I looked at him, but I didn't know how to stop myself from oozing with adoration for him.

It wasn't just that he was gorgeous. I mean, he was—but that wasn't the point. Javier hated the CEO of Child Motors probably more than everyone else in the company, and that was hot in itself.

Mostly because Javier was a Child. His father owned the luxury car company in which we worked but you wouldn't know it, partially because George Child treated his only son worse than most of us, but also because Javvy was simply likeable. No one would ever suspect that he was brought up in private jets and yachts, fed caviar, and treated to spring breaks in Belize.

But maybe he didn't live like that? It was hard to know considering that his job was barely a step above mine. There was a rumor that he had started working in the mailroom the year he turned sixteen, and at twenty-six, he was just middle management, still clawing his way up the ranks.

I handed him the coffee in a mug which read THIS MIGHT BE VODKA, and he grinned at me, a sheepish look on his face.

"You must think I'm a real tool," he sighed. "Bitching about stuff like this."

My dark eyebrows shot up, and I shook my head in denial.

"I don't think you're a tool at all!" I blubbered, again hating myself for spewing my words out all in one gush.

"You may not believe this, but I get paid the same way everyone else around here does. This insurance thing affects me too."

I had not known that.

The information made him all the more intriguing, but before I could open my mouth to press him on the way his family business operated, a sharp tone caused me to turn toward the door.

"Must be nice to flirt all day while the rest of us pick up your slack, Aura."

"Coming, Steph," I mumbled, realizing that she did have a point. My "break" had lasted a lot longer than ten minutes.

Steph grunted and stomped off, leaving me to glance apologetically at Javvy.

"Duty calls," I chuckled even though my heart was pounding.

"Yeah, don't worry," he replied. "Kevin will be down here barking at me in a minute, too. Thanks for the coffee."

He raised it in silent toast toward me, and I nodded, shifting my eyes shyly downward.

"See you later."

I hated the way I said that, my tone almost petulant. I didn't want to leave but I couldn't very well stay and hang out with Javier Child all day long. If they were making cuts, I wasn't high enough on the food chain to be playing games. And God knew, I needed that job. My writing career hadn't panned out the way I'd hoped.

It also helps if you actually write the novel you want to be published, I reminded myself, thinking about the half-written manuscript buried in my closet.

"Hey, Aura..."

I paused in the doorway and studied his handsome face.

"Hm?"

"Listen, I—" He stopped speaking as if trying to collect his thoughts before he uttered another word. I stared at him curiously. I couldn't imagine what would tie Javvy's tongue. Even as I thought it, a rush of heat warmed my crotch as the memory of his very skilled tongue flooded my mind in an instant.

"I just wanted to say that what happened at the Christmas party..." he trailed off again, and I turned so red, I was sure the expression frozen on my face resembled Grimace from McDonald's.

"Don't worry about it," I breathed, wishing he had not ruined a perfectly good moment between us. Why was he bringing that up now?

"No!" he choked, his own cheeks staining. "I mean to say that what happened between us at the Christmas party was amazing. I know we never really talked about it after it happened, but I've thought about you. A lot."

That, I had not been expecting. It had never really occurred to me that the drunken escapade of heavy petting and intoxicated kisses had meant anything to him.

It wasn't that I considered Javvy a playboy. I didn't really know him enough to have an opinion on his personal life. How much could I glean about a guy who I only passed in the hall day to day or bumped into at break or lunch? Still, he didn't strike me as the type to spread his seed with any woman dazzled by his last name.

Even so, I didn't think there was anything more appealing about me than say, oh, a thousand other women I could think of off the top of my head. I wasn't being self-deprecating; it was a fact.

I was by no means a raving beauty although I did have my charms: a brilliant white smile and intense green eyes that shone like cut beryl.

Against my almost black waves and naturally olive tone, I could be very alluring in the right light. But we lived in California, and the competition was fierce.

"I have completely humiliated myself, haven't I?" he muttered, turning away. "I didn't mean to put you on the spot. I just—"

"No!" I gasped, snapping back into the strange reality in which I found myself. "No, I...I'm glad you said something. I...I've thought about you too."

The words tried to stick in my throat, but I managed to force them out as I smiled nervously.

"Honestly, I wanted to ask you out afterward, in the New Year, but..." he cleared his throat and looked up at me, his steely eyes boring into mine. "Let me just be honest. My dad has been making my life miserable since I broke off my relationship with the daughter of some oil tycoon he was in cahoots with. She didn't take it well either and suddenly, I was being double-teamed by two of the biggest psychopaths on the planet."

The confession was certainly stunning, more so because it was the most he'd ever disclosed to me at once that the nature of the topic.

"I... I'm sorry to hear that," I managed to say, and he grunted, shaking his head.

"Okay, I'm not very good at this," he sighed. "I didn't mean to regale you with the minutia of my personal turmoil. I am actually trying to ask you out."

My mouth gaped open, and I was nodding even before I realized I was doing it.

"Yeah." I replied, happiness tickling me as it crept up and down my spine. "Yeah, I'd like that. Let me give you my number."

I extended my hand for his cell, but Javier hung his head guiltily downward.

"I already took it from your personnel file."

I knew I should have been somewhat annoyed, but I was completely flattered by the gesture. I wondered how long he'd been holding onto it.

"Are you completely turned off now?"

He sounded like he expected my answer to be a resounding "HELL YES," but how could I be? For almost two months, I had been secretly pining for the boss's son, and here he was, handing himself to me on a silver platter.

"Nope," I answered. "Make sure you use it."

He looked back up, his charismatic smile illuminating his features.

"You free tonight?"

"Not anymore."

Our eyes locked and a familiar sexual thrill slithered through me. Javier was finally going to finish what he started.

2

CHAPTER TWO

JAVVY

"Where have you been?"

The question was fired out at me like a spray of buckshot. Dad's words shouldn't have stopped me cold in my tracks. After all, he always sounded indignant, furious, and condescending.

Yet, like the trained poodle he designed me to be, I stopped and turned to face him through the study doors which were conspicuously open.

Since when was the iron door ever ajar, let alone open? I couldn't remember a time in my life that I had ever seen the double doors leading into my father's private man cave open. Certainly not both of them as if he was airing out the smell of a dead body. I wouldn't put it past him, and I didn't have a good feeling.

"Work. You should try it some time," I shot back, and his blue-grey eyes hardened into sheets of ice, which was difficult for them to do, considering they were always the coldest orbs I'd ever known.

"Get. In. Here."

Uh oh. He was annunciating his syllables. More foreshadowing of bad to come.

"What is it, Dad?" I grunted, stalking toward him, already trying to keep my temper in check. I'd been stuck catching up on inventory, a job which belonged to Kevin, my supervisor. Unfortunately for me, Kevin was a favorite of my dad's and enjoyed sticking the screws to me. He seemed to think that good things were coming for him if he tortured me. Hence the endless pile of work which was not mine.

I'd been tempted to do it half-assed or worse, to set Kevin up for stealing parts. If inventory was missing, Kevin was technically responsible, but something told me that it would be me taking the blame anyway. It was hardly worth entertaining.

"Sit down."

"Dad, I have a date tonight. Whatever it is, can it wait?"

Obviously, it couldn't, but I couldn't resist sticking my date in his face.

George snorted and sat back against the high leather back of his chair.

"You've got some nerve after what you did to Emily."

"Oh my God! If this is about Emily—"

"Shut up and listen," George snarled. "Something happened, and I need your help."

Again, I was taken aback by his word choice.

Is he drunk?

I leaned forward slightly to peer into his face, but I don't know who I was kidding; even if he was completely off his face, I'd never know it. He was far too seasoned a functional alcoholic for me to tell.

The president and CEO of one of the most valuable car brands in the world is a lush. I wonder how many DUIs he's had stricken from his record.

"Alvin got arrested for insider trading and embezzlement."

A laugh escaped my lips. I hadn't meant to snicker, but I thought he was making a tasteless joke. After all, Alvin Selmy was the VP of operations at Child Motors and Dad's righthand man. I pictured Al in his too-tight, trademark English-cut suit, face pinched in British distain. He was impossibly proper. Even in my mind's eye, I was describing him with an accent.

He's Lane Pryce from Mad Men for Christ's sake. There's no way...

Yet as I stared at my father, I saw that he was not kidding, not in the least. I reminded myself quickly what happened to Lane Pryce and reconsidered my original assessment.

Dad's not drunk; he's livid.

"Oh shit, Dad..."

"'Oh shit' is right, Javier. They took him to Folsom this afternoon."

My eyes bugged, and I sat forward further.

"Already? He's been convicted?"

My father nodded, reaching across the lacquered desk for a pack of cigarettes. I had no idea he'd started smoking again, but if there was ever a time...

"Jesus, Dad! How did you manage to keep this out of the press for months? It's been months, hasn't it? This is huge news!"

"In due time, Javier, if you play your cards right, I will give you all the secrets along with the keys to the kingdom," he replied, inhaling a Marlborough deeply before exhaling the smoke from between his lips.

"What are you going to do?"

George took another deep inhale and shook his thinning blonde hair. I was reminded of a time when he was considered a handsome man, but it was difficult to remember why people thought that.

And everyone says I look just like him. What does that say for my future?

Aside from my exotic name, I inherited no traits from my mother, a Salvadorian immigrant left penniless by my father after their divorce ten years ago.

The conflict between my mom and I was clear: she had wanted me to live with her in San Fernando Valley but George had other ideas, ones that did not include me staying connected with Mom.

"The kingdom could be yours," my dad would whisper in my ear. "You just have to earn it. But if you go to your mother, you will lose it all, I swear."

I believed him then. I was sixteen. What the hell did I know? I hadn't studied history enough to know that every narcissist needs an audience. He would have withered and died if he didn't have me "learning" from his wisdom.

It had been Dad's idea to start me at the bottom, pulling me out of school to work at Child Motors. In the back of my mind, I'd always wondered if he'd change his mind someday and decide to boot me out anyway. What would I do then?

I knew I could probably start over, get a GED or something equally as humiliating, but I would probably run home to my mom with my tail between my legs, telling her that she was right all along.

It hadn't happened nor had George ever suggested it, but my doubts about him lingered, overshadowing my every move. I knew my father. He was a sadist by nature.

Suddenly, I realized why he had called me into the office.

He was going to promote me to vice president.

A mixture of nervousness and excitement filled my gut as I contemplated what that would mean. Selmy lived part-time in the UK and part-time here, but that didn't mean I'd have to, did it?

Instantly, I thought of Aura and my heart sank. It had taken me two months to build up the nerve to ask her out.

She's going to think I'm jerking her around if I tell her I'm leaving for London. ...unless she comes with me...

That was something to consider. Would she be weirded out if I asked her or would she think it was romantic? It was hard to tell. Aura was a little mysterious, unlike any woman I'd ever met.

What I had told her that day in the breakroom was true: George had been on a warpath about Emily, and the girl herself was a maniac. She was showing up everywhere I went and hanging around the house at night. It didn't take me long to figure out that she was working with George to rekindle our relationship.

Emily's idea of romance was boiled bunny, I suppose.

I knew that begging or threatening my father would not work. Instead, I got him drunk one night and told him "in confidence" that I was scared of Emily and going to the police for a restraining order. Of course, he had no way of knowing that I was onto his role in the scheme.

George told me to sleep on it, and as I had foreseen, Emily disappeared. I waited three weeks to be sure before telling my dad I knew what he'd done and thanking him for ridding me of the problem. He was madder than hell, but Emily had already moved onto her next victim.

Aura is completely the opposite. After our little date in the cloakroom, she didn't go all crazy. She's too self-confident, too classy for shit like that. I'd love to take her with me to Europe.

"Are you listening to a Goddamned word I'm saying?"

"Of course, Dad."

"So, I'm promoting you," he continued, and I felt a burst in my chest. I couldn't be sure if it was good or bad, but it was there, and I felt it.

"I e-mailed Jake and told him that you're taking over as of Monday."

"Jake who?" My mind went blank as I tried to remember someone in England named Jake.

George eyed me with annoyance.

"Jake Lucette. You really haven't been listening at all, have you?"

"I have!" I protested, completely lost. "I just missed the part about Jake."

"Jake Lucette is the head of operations in your building. I'm making Jake the new VP. You're taking over his job. Christ, don't make me regret my decision already, Javier."

"What?" I choked. "You're giving the job to Jake Lucette? That man is a boot-licking prick!"

George's mouth curled into a cruel smile, and he shook his head.

"You thought I would simply hand over a position like that to you? You can't even pay attention when I'm speaking. Try not to fuck this up, Javvy."

"Dad!" I grunted. "Jake has only been with the company four years. What the hell does he know about running..."

I stopped myself, realizing that George was probably enjoying every second of my anger.

Every move he makes is calculated, controlled. He loves watching you jump and grow hot under the collar, but I'm not falling into the same trap this time. Screw you, Dad. I have a beautiful woman waiting for my call.

Remembering that I didn't have to leave Aura behind was suddenly the silver lining I almost missed, and a genuine smile broke over my face, apparently baffling my father.

"Is something funny?" he asked casually, but I could see him wracking his brain as to what I might have to grin about.

"I told you," I replied, spinning to leave him alone with his wicked tendencies. "I have a date."

I slammed the double doors closed in my wake and stalked toward the back stairs leading to my suite in the east wing. I wouldn't let the conversation I'd had with George put a damper on my mood. I'd spent two long months fantasizing about Aura Cameron's full mouth, remembering the way she'd tasted. Her kisses tasted like apple martinis and her hands curved around every aspect of my body as if she knew me better than I knew myself.

My pants were suddenly very snug around the crotch, and I pulled my cell from my back pocket, scrolling as I made my way upstairs.

"Hello?" She sounded breathless as if she'd run for the phone.

"Hey. It's me." I don't know why I expected her to know who "me" was, but she did. Instantly.

"Hi," she purred, unmistakably happy to hear from me.

"You still good for tonight?"

"I'm good. You good?"

"Never better. I'm just having a shower and changing. Can you text me your address?"

"You didn't steal that from my file, too?" she teased, and I turned red. I hadn't but I knew I'd crossed a line by filching her phone number.

"I swear, I didn't. If you're uncomfortable—"

"What time will you be here to pick me up?"

I relaxed, knowing that she got off on taunting me, and that was fine. I was happy to get Aura off any which way she wanted.

CHAPTER THREE
AURA

I had no idea why I was so nervous. After all, I'd already stuck my tongue down this guy's throat, and we'd seen one another a bunch of times since then.

But in the shadowy light of the passing streetlamps, I found myself peering at him through my peripheral vision as if I was seeing him for the first time.

Goddamn, he's handsome. Even with his jaw so tense. I wonder what's on his mind?

I could have flattered myself that he was thinking about our impending date, but I knew better. He was upset about something, even though he was trying to hide it. I don't know how I could be so sure, but sometimes I felt like I'd known Javvy forever. We seemed to just click on an almost psychic level.

"Penny for your thoughts?"

Where the hell did that stupid line come from? What is this? 1954?

To my relief, he turned to look at me, slowing the car at a red light and stopping fully before sighing deeply.

"My dad is a prick."

Oh.

How else was I supposed to answer that? I mean, it was really common knowledge among all the employees at Child Motors. It wasn't like I could vehemently deny it. Anyway, Javvy wasn't looking for a denial. He was angry and wanted confirmation.

"I've heard he can be difficult," I offered, unsure of what else to say on the matter. I couldn't very well trash talk the CEO to his son... could I? It wasn't a chance I was willing to take.

"No, he's not difficult, he's a horse's ass, and I despise him."

I reached out and touched his tense forearm as he clutched the gearshift as if he were driving stick even though the car was automatic.

"What happened?" I asked softly.

"He..." The light turned green and Javvy shot forward, the power of the Windchaser causing me to lurch forward. It was the cheapest make of the Child line, but it was still an eighty-thousand-dollar car, even if it was seven years old.

"I can't really discuss it," he muttered, seeming annoyed that he had to say that. "It doesn't matter anyway. It isn't news that he's a prick."

"Why can't you discuss it?" I was more curious than anything. It sounded like Javvy had been sworn to secrecy or something, and I was intrigued. The dynamic between father and son was one I didn't understand in the least, but I was hardly one to judge; my mother had been a tyrant, too, before she died.

"Do you mind if I just pull over for a second?"

I was surprised, but I nodded quickly as I saw the deep stress in his face. We were going to be late for our dinner reservation, but I didn't care. Suddenly, I wasn't hungry anyway. He obviously needed to get whatever he had to say off his chest, and I wasn't going to stop him.

Javvy steered the Windchaser into the entrance of a park, guiding the luxury car into the seclusion of the forested parking lot. In seconds, we were hidden behind a wall of coniferous trees, blocking Sierra Road.

I hadn't realized we had driven into the quiet area of San Jose until I saw we were in Alum Rock Park. There were no other cars around, the darkness threatening to overcome the meager light of the lot's streetlamps as Javvy turned off the car.

"Sorry," he muttered. "I don't know why I let him get to me like this. It's not like it's new or something."

A pang of compassion filled my bones, and I stared at him as he collected his thoughts. It didn't take him long, and he looked at me apologetically.

"God, listen to me. We're on a date, and I'm whining about my dad like a pissed off teenager."

"You're not whining," I replied gently. "You're getting something out of your system. It sounds a lot more serious than Daddy not giving you the keys to the Ferrari."

He grinned wickedly at her jest.

"Childs don't driver Ferraris, Miss Cameron," he said in a nasally voice as if mimicking one of his father's upperclassman friends. "We only travel in Child motor vehicles. Shame on you for suggesting otherwise."

"Pardon my ignorance, Your Highness," I chuckled, and I realized that my hand was still on his forearm, but he made no move to take it away.

Our eyes met, and he shook his head ruefully.

"My father pretends that everything he does is to teach me how to run the company, but when the opportunity arises to give me power, he squashes me, and I swear, Aura, he loves it when he does."

"I'm sure that's not true," I said softly, squeezing his bare skin gently. His blue eyes traveled to where my fingers curled over his skin, and he looked back up at me.

"I'm such an idiot talking about this," he muttered, his tone like gravel as he leaned forward. He must have read the desire in my eyes, and I was glad. The heat surging through my body told me that if he didn't act quickly, I would be forced to pin him back against the leather of the driver's seat—but that I would be the one doing all the riding.

I didn't have to act, my eyes melded into his as he covered the short distance between us across the center console.

Our lips clashed and instantly I was filled with a familiar pang, one which I had grown to know quite well in the past weeks. The difference was, this time my longing for Javier Child was being fulfilled in person, not in the halls of my imagination.

His palms cupped my face, drawing me closer to him, our tongues teasing at the tip. Bolts of electricity slid through me, one after another, and my own arms moved up to pull him toward me.

I knew what was coming, and I fumbled along the side of the car, sliding the seat fully back to allot him the room I knew he was going to need.

He wasted no time, his muscled frame half-slipped over the barrier of the seats, his leg slinging over the gearshift to land on the passenger's side. In seconds, he had maneuvered his whole body onto mine without losing his position on my lips.

He's done this before was my first thought, but I shoved it aside, knowing I was only trying to ruin the goodness of the moment for myself with fatalistic thoughts.

Not everyone in life will disappoint you, I chided myself as Javvy pushed my legs apart, his knees pressed against the floor mat.

I broke off the kiss when I felt his hands caress the tops of my breasts over the low cut of my simple but tight black dress.

I had opted for casual but sexy—or at least that was the look I was going for. A part of me just felt slutty as the skirt rode up higher on my hips, resting there against the red silk of my panties.

Javvy's face nuzzled into my bosom, his breath causing goose-bumps to explode over my body.

"God, you feel so good," I mumbled. "I'm so glad we're doing this."

He chuckled softly, easing my breasts from the material, exposing my nipple for his lips to explore with his tongue. Sparks flooded me from stem to stern, my thighs growing damp as he latched on, nibbling and sucking at me with delicious vigor.

I bucked my body upward, wanting to make contact with his hardness. I remembered how it had felt in the coatroom at the Piazza.

Had the alcohol made him seem bigger or was really as huge as he'd felt to my touch that night?

As if sensing my intention, he rose up higher, his heavy form pinning me against the seat, and I could see he was uncomfortable, but before I could offer to switch positions with him, the seat fell back, and we were horizontal.

"That's better," he chuckled, his lips meeting mine again. Now I could feel the telltale bulge in his crotch, and I was hot. Too hot.

"Is that all you?" I choked, my eyes widening as I pushed my hips urgently upward, grinding my swollen button against the material of his pants.

He lifted his head from my chest again, his eyes gleaming as he licked his lips.

"Wanna find out?"

I exhaled slowly, nodding like an excited kid. "Oh, yes, please," I moaned.

Javvy smiled at my response, his hand reaching for his belt, and I jumped in to help. To my embarrassment, my hands were shaking in anticipation, but I don't think he noticed.

Oh my God! Is that all going to fit inside me?

I didn't have a very good vantage point from where I lay but my hands smoothed along his length. His veins were ridged, and I trailed my fingers against him as if I was reading braille.

"Are you okay?" he murmured, his eyes boring into mine as he positioned the tip of his throbbing unit against my drenched lower lips. Suddenly I couldn't find my voice, but I could still nod, even though I wasn't sure if I could take him.

He seemed to sense my hesitation, and he kept his head sliding up and down against me, but I couldn't take it anymore; if he continued on that path, I'd release before he got inside me.

I raised my thighs up, pressing them tightly against either side of his hips, and I felt the tip of him glide inside me unexpectedly. Javvy seemed as surprised as I was.

"Are you sure you're okay?"

I looked at him, breathlessly biting down on my lower lip. I was certain I'd never been so wet in my life.

"Take me," I begged, my voice barely above a whisper. Javvy did not need a second plea and slowly, he fell into me, expanding my entrance with his huge member.

I gasped, but he went slowly, his beautiful eyes fixed on mine as if trying to gauge my comfort level, but as he moved slowly, I found I needed him to work with more urgency. The fire inside me was growing, sweeping through my gut and bolting through my core at a pace he was not matching.

I knew he was worried about hurting me, but I didn't care. I needed him deep and fast.

My fingers dug into his bare cheeks and again, I jerked upward to meet his full length, once more choking at the unexpected girth of him.

Who knew they made men this way? Not me.

He acknowledged my desire and instantly, his movements became more intense until he was completely inside me, filling me where I'd never been touched before.

I couldn't stifle my cries of pleasure-filled pain, but he didn't slow down, his grunts growing louder as he lowered his face to my ear.

"You're so tight, so hot," he gasped, his words blending together as his cock became a steel rod inside me.

I yelped, the stabbing driving me to exactly where I needed to be.

"D-don't...s-stop!" I managed to squeak out, but I don't think he heard me as he continued to plunge inside me. He was far too close to his own release to notice the gush of heat emanating from between my thighs.

I screamed out as I climaxed, nails digging into his back as I spilled, but I had not quite finished when I was met with searing streams of his own release.

Our juices intermingling, legs tensing and clenching against one another until finally, our spasms diminished, and we lay in a shaking pile of arms and legs.

Sweat had broken out over my face, and I could feel the sting of the saline as it dripped down my forehead and into my eyes but Javvy lay firmly across me, making moving impossible.

I could have asked him to adjust himself, but I didn't want to ruin this buzzy, sultry feeling. I felt like we had melted into one another in those moments, become one—

"Oh shit! Someone's coming!"

He bolted upright as a flash of headlights filled the car, and I giggled nervously, hoping it wasn't a cop.

He fumbled on the floor for his pants as the lights faded away toward the far end of the parking lot, the red taillights barely visible in the fogged up Windchaser.

"Sorry," he said sheepishly, yanking on his trousers. "It's been a long time since I've made out in a car. I didn't mean to react so nervously."

I was trying to remember if I'd ever made out in a car. I certainly had never had sex in one. I'd spent my childhood trying to provide for me and Alex, with romance the absolute last thing on my mind.

"I'm not sorry in the least," I replied, grinning at him as I smoothed down my dress.

He offered me a return grin, doing up his belt and then glancing at his cell phone. His smile faded as his brow puckered.

"We missed our reservation at Morton's. We'll never get in without one on a Friday night."

"Morton's?"

He eyed me as he managed to find his way back into the driver's seat.

"Yeah, why? You don't like steak?"

"I don't like anything that costs a hundred bucks and leaves me hungry," I replied sincerely although I wasn't sure that was the case. I'd never actually eaten at the five-star restaurant. When would I have? Idly, I wondered if he could even afford Morton's on what his father paid him, but I was too polite to ask.

Javvy guffawed and gave me an appreciative look. He started the car, the defogger blasting.

"I was trying to impress you," he confessed but I already knew that.

"You did impress me."

Our gazes met, and we were silent for a minute.

"Well," Javvy said. "I don't know about you but I'm hungrier than I was before. What should we do for dinner?"

I shrugged.

"There's a Wendy's on Capitol," I suggested, and his mouth gaped slightly.

"How did you know I was craving a Baconator?"

I had no way of knowing if that was true or if he was teasing me, so I snickered and turned away.

"Kismet maybe?"

"Maybe," he agreed quietly and in such a way that made me sneak another look at him. He was still staring at me.

4
_____

CHAPTER FOUR
JAVVY

We fit together so naturally that I couldn't remember a time when Aura wasn't in my life. I could kick myself for not having asked her out sooner, but I couldn't do much about the past. All I could do was look forward to the future, to our future together.

I spent more time at her apartment in Milpitas than I did at home, and I was grateful to have an escape from my father. Whenever I did see him, whether I stopped in the sprawling estate for a change of clothes or if he popped into the office, I could feel the tension between us. He didn't say much to me, as if he considered me a brat for being upset.

"Is this a hotel?" he barked at me one evening when I let myself into the mansion. "You come and go as you please?"

My eyes narrowed, and I stared at him balefully.

"I would have moved out five years ago if you'd let me," I reminded him. "I didn't realize that I had a curfew."

George snickered.

"You really are more like a daughter, aren't you? I'm glad I didn't give you the VP position. You have no idea what it's like to be in power, to be—"

"You know what, Dad?" I interrupted, not wanting to hear another word out of his smug mouth. "I don't give a shit. I don't even want this company anymore. You can find someone else to take it over."

I spun to take the stairs two at a time, but his voice rang out, following me.

"Be careful what you wish for, Javier, or you just might get it!"

I'll admit that in that moment, I sincerely hoped he would find someone else. I was sick of it all, and the more time I spent with Aura, the more I realized exactly how much better life could be without him.

We'd been inseparable for nearly a month, and while she hadn't formally invited me to move in with her, I was there all the time anyway. It just seemed like the right thing to do—like we were going in that direction anyway.

I rushed into my suite and threw my duffle bag on the bed, before wandering into the full closet off the sitting area of my room.

You're almost twenty-seven years old. Why are you still living here?

It was time to move out, for sure. I couldn't live under my dad's thumb forever, no matter how he played it.

My cell chimed, and I reached for it.

"Hey babe," I answered, seeing Aura's number. "What's up?"

"I was thinking Indian for supper," she replied. "That work for you?"

"I was thinking you for supper."

"You had me for lunch. And breakfast."

I sighed into the phone although I was grinning like an idiot.

"But you're my favorite meal," I whined playfully. "Why you gotta be like that?"

"How's it going over there?" she asked, and I could hear the concern in her voice. I'd opened up to her about the relationship between my father and me, even though I knew it was probably disloyal, considering she was a secretary at the company. Yet I knew I could trust Aura. She had nothing to gain by repeating it even if she wanted to.

"Same shit," I answered lightly, but even I could hear the edge in my voice.

"Just come home," she urged. "Forget about him."

"I'm on my way!" I replied, feeling a rush of heat course through me as she said "home."

She thinks of us as living together, too, I realized, and I was filled with elation. I'd never been with anyone who evoked feelings like this in me.

"I have to talk to you about something," she added, and the smile froze on my face.

"What's wrong?" I asked, instantly sensing the worry in her tone. "What happened?"

"No, nothing!" she insisted. "We'll discuss it when you get home."

"Now I'm freaking out! Tell me!"

"Oh my God, Javvy. It's not a big deal. It's just...my landlord upped the rent, and my car insurance went up. I had to get a new alternator last month and—"

"Do you need some money?" I asked, and I heard her suck air in through her teeth.

"Not from you." Her words were like ice. "I'm taking on a bartending job at El Chapo's."

"Wait, what?" I asked, shocked by the news. "You can't!"

"*I can't?*" she echoed. "Why *can't* I?"

I should have shut up right then and there, but I couldn't stop myself, it seemed.

"Because if you work nights, I'll never see you!"

I knew how stupid and selfish it sounded, and really, that wasn't what I'd meant to say at all. I wanted to tell her that I would give her money if she needed it. After all, my promotion had come with a sizeable raise. I wanted to tell her that we could move in together and split the bills. Instead, I came across like some jealous, petty boyfriend who didn't want to miss out on my tail time.

"That's why I'm giving you the heads up now," she said shortly. "We'll work it out."

I exhaled in a whoosh.

"We'll talk when I get home," I told her, and she gave a small laugh.

"Isn't that what I said in the first place?"

"I need to start listening to you a bit better."

"You continue to talk out of your ass. I gotta go order dinner. Hurry back. I'm horny." The call disconnected in my ear, and I turned back to my packing.

At least she's not mad.

It was just one of the million things I loved about Aura. She never stayed mad or held grudges. She just forgave and forgot—not that we fought about anything.

I eyed the closet, a room in itself, the perimeter filled with shirts and pants inside cedar cupboards. There was an entire wall of shoes, a different pair for any situation. Eyeing it all, I began to regard it all a little differently, as somewhat wasteful.

The rich don't even like nice things. They just need tax write-offs. There is no one in the world who needs this much stuff.

Suddenly, I grabbed a suitcase from the back of the closet and began to fill it. Screw waiting to discuss it. I was going to march right into Aura's apartment with all my belongings and put her on the spot.

She won't be as apt to say no if I appear like this, will she?

I guess I'd find out.

I hauled the first filled case out of the closet and set it near the door and was dutifully working on the second when I heard my name being called.

"Javier!"

I didn't need to look—obviously it was my father.

"What is it, Dad?"

"What are you doing? Are you going on vacation?" He stood with his hands on his hips and his eyebrows beetled over his scowl.

I sat back on my heels and looked at him, pursing my lips together. If I told him I intended to move in with someone, and Aura refused me, I'd be back at the house that night with my tail between my legs. It was better if I didn't say anything until I knew I was sure.

"Just getting rid of some stuff," I lied. "What are you doing up here?"

It was odd to see him in my bedroom. He never came in, but I realized that my earlier words to him must have affected him.

He's been downstairs stewing, I realized, the smile on my face becoming difficult to swallow.

George didn't answer me right away, turning his back to look around the suite as if he was seeing it for the first time.

"Who is this woman you're seeing?"

"Her name is Aura Cameron. She works at the San Jose office."

"In what capacity?"

"She's a secretary in Admin."

My father snorted as if I'd told him I was dating a crack whore.

"Sounds ambitious."

I ground my teeth together and checked my temper. Going after Aura was not going to end well for him.

"At least she works," I retorted, the dig entirely directed his way. I couldn't remember the last time I'd seen him at the office for any reason. It was like he just expected the company to run itself while he went golfing and schmoozing.

George's head whipped around, his steely eyes narrowing dangerously.

"What have you told her about our family affairs?"

I scoffed, returning to my task.

"What family? What affairs?"

"Don't be petulant, Javier. It doesn't suit you."

"I don't know what you're asking, Dad!" I snapped back. "What are you going on about?"

"Did you tell her about Alvin Selmy?"

Oh...

I turned my head, pretending to busy myself with my chore but not quickly enough, and he caught the flush on my face.

"What the hell is wrong with you, Javier? How could you tell—"

"I didn't tell her shit," I snapped. "Stop talking to me like I'm a five year old."

"Stop acting like you're a five year old!"

I stared at him for a long moment, realizing, albeit not for the first time, that that was exactly as he saw me—a little boy who needed reprimanding. I made my decision in that minute.

"Dad, I'm moving out," I said flatly, making my decision as we stood. "I'm twenty-seven years old, and you treat me like an infant who can't wipe his own ass."

"Well, if you weren't constantly disappointing me, Javier, I wouldn't have to treat you like that, would I?"

I smirked mirthlessly.

"I guess you're right," I replied, refusing to take the bait. I'd been goaded by him enough in my life. He had shown me how much he valued me when he had promoted Jake to VP. There was no need for me to stick around, especially when I was 90 percent sure that Dad had no intention of passing the company along to me anyway.

"Javier, you're just not ready," he growled, clearly annoyed that I wouldn't engage with him. "You have no grit, no fire—"

"Yeah, I got it, Dad." I snapped the locks on the second case and pulled it out of the closet. There was still another small case to be loaded, but I was afraid if I stuck around any longer, the urge to punch my father in his face would overwhelm me.

"I don't want the company."

I said the words as flatly as I could, but I knew there was emotion in them and if I heard it, so did my dad. Of course, I wanted the damned company. It was why I'd stayed around for so long, why I'd given up the relationship with my mother. Walking away from it all would mean the last ten years had been for nothing.

The smile which formed on his lips was cold and cruel.

"All right," he replied, spinning on his heel to leave me in the sitting room. "I'll have my will changed in the morning."

I stood there, watching him walk away, and my stomach flipped with anxiety.

He's just talking shit. He's not going to cut you out of the will...is he?

Who knew what he would do? Predictability was not a quality which George possessed.

I had no choice but to stick to my guns and move forward. What was really going to change? My whole life I'd been working at the company, not running it. It wasn't as if my situation was going to change if I never got something that I never had.

And I have Aura. What the hell else do I want?

With new resolve, I gathered my packed bags and pulled them into the hallway.

Screw the company and screw you, Dad. I'm already happier than you'll ever be.

CHAPTER FIVE
AURA

I could feel trouble brewing before it happened. Call it a sixth sense but I knew something was about to disrupt our growing happiness.

Maybe it was starting the second job and seeing less of Javvy, despite him basically living in my cramped one-bedroom apartment. He hadn't officially moved in, but he barely ever went home.

I suspected that George Child was giving him a fair amount of grief about it, but my lover never said anything about it to me. He was determined to make our budding relationship flourish, even though Javvy brought up his father with less frequency than he had before.

That morning, I was studying him across the kitchen island, a mug of coffee in my hand as the remnants of sleep still stubbornly clung to me. I'd worked at the office during the days and the evenings at El Chapo's. It was a decent enough gig and not nearly as bad as I had expected it to be. There wasn't as much groping as I remembered when I'd served in college. Either times had changed or El Chapo's was just higher class. Either way, I wasn't looking a gift horse in the mouth.

Javvy's face was glued to his tablet, and I could see he was just as sleepy as I was. I wondered if he had waited up for me, even though he seemed sound asleep when I got home.

Probably, I mused, shaking my head. He'd done it the first three shifts I'd worked, and I gave him hell for doing it.

"I'm a grown woman, Javvy. I don't need a babysitter." My tone had been exasperated, but secretly I was flattered by his attentiveness. He was the true definition of a gentleman, and I loved him more every day. I could hardly believe that he was even better than I imagined. When had I ever met a man who didn't disappoint me in some way?

"Okay," he replied as if he could tell fighting with me wouldn't accomplish anything.

I opened my mouth to ask him what depressing news he was reading. Judging by the expression on his face, I could see it was something political but before I could say anything, my cell rang.

It was my turn for my brow to crease as I peered at my cell. Who could be calling at that hour?

"Who is that?" Javvy asked, mimicking my thoughts.

"My brother."

I snatched my Android off the counter and accepted the call.

"Hey."

"Hey," Alex chirped. "Long time no talk."

"It's seven o'clock in the morning. Have you not slept yet?"

Alex chuckled, a low, sonorous sound which almost seemed sober, but I knew my kid brother better than that.

"Is that your way of asking if I'm drunk dialing you?"

"Of course not!" I denied, cringing at my own lie. "I'm glad to hear your voice, Alex. Where are you?"

"In Tijuana."

I blinked.

"Why? Oh...Alex, what did you do?" I felt a knot forming in my stomach. There was no way I had enough money to bail him out of a Mexican prison. Alex howled at my tone.

"I'm staying with Dad," he replied. "Relax!"

Is that supposed to make me feel better?

A bubble of discontent rocked my stomach as I thought about my father. After my mom had died, he had been more than clear; he wanted nothing to do with raising two teenagers. He'd had little choice but to open his home to us, but that didn't mean he was happy about it.

I'd hightailed it out of there at first opportunity, busting my butt to finish my associate degree at college before working a string of menial jobs, and eventually Alex had followed suit—leaving that is—but not going to school or working. He'd fallen into a pit of drunken depression. For a year, he'd stayed with me until his drinking binges disrupted my life too much for me to bear, and I'd been forced to throw him out too.

I'd tried to get him into government-sponsored rehab. Neither of us had money for the good kind of rehab, and soon he was back on the streets again, couch surfing and living off the kindness of others in the same position as he. Eventually he'd found his way back to me, but it had only lasted a month the last time.

That was eight months ago. This was the first time I was hearing his voice. I was both relieved and stressed by it.

"How's that going, Alex?" I asked cautiously, wondering if he was calling because he wanted to come back to me. Even if I wanted him to stay, which I didn't, I just didn't have the room. I had Javvy to think about.

Inadvertently, I glanced at my boyfriend who was watching me curiously, and I forced a fake smile at him, but it was clear that he could hear the tension in my words. I shifted my eyes back to the counter.

"Actually, things are going really good, sis. Dad and I were talking about you last night, and I realized that we hadn't left things really good between us. I thought I'd call and see how you're doing."

I didn't want to feel suspicious of him, but I couldn't help it.

"Things are good, Al. I—" I stopped myself from telling him about Javvy. Somehow any good news I had to share with my family would get tainted in some way.

What is that quote? "Travel and tell no one. Live a true love story and tell no one. Live happily and tell no one. People ruin beautiful things."

"Things are good," I concluded lamely. "How long have you been staying at Dad's?"

"A little over a month now. He's got a girlfriend who once had a substance abuse problem. She helped me detox and get clean. I'm three weeks sober."

I loathed the cynicism coursing through my veins, but I had heard this before. Both the "new girlfriend" and the "I'm clean" spiels.

"That's great news," I managed. "I'm really happy for both of you."

Alex laughed as if he could hear the skepticism.

"I know, I know," he grunted. "You've heard it all before, but it's true this time. And I think this lady is 'the one' for Dad. You should come and meet her. Her name is Cate and—"

"Sorry, Alex. I'm working two jobs now, and I really don't have much time to myself."

"Two jobs?" he echoed. "What about your novel?"

I felt my back tense, and I gulped back the bile filling my throat. I wanted to scream at my brother that life wasn't that simple, that I couldn't just drop everything to pursue my passion, hoping for the best.

"It's on hold," I replied lightly. "But tell Dad and Cate I wish them the best of luck."

Alex sighed deeply.

"You're so talented, Aura. You've always been the brains of this family. You should focus on your writing and—"

"Listen, Alex, I've gotta get ready for work, okay?"

"It's Saturday!" he protested. "You work every day?"

"Yep. Gotta go. Thanks for calling and stay in touch."

I disconnected the call before he could say anything else, but my heart was beating furiously.

Why is it always like that when I talk to him or Dad? It drains me.

"You're not really working today, are you?" Javvy demanded.

"Not until four," I assured him. "I just didn't want to talk anymore."

"Is he drunk?"

My head jerked up, and I glanced at Javvy warily. I didn't remember telling him about Alex's drinking problem, but I must have. There was little I didn't talk to him about. Still, I was defensive.

"No," I replied quickly. "He sounds sober. He's staying with my dad in Mexico."

Javvy cocked his head to the side pensively.

"You're worried," he offered, and I grunted.

"He's twenty-two years old, Javvy. I'm not his babysitter. If he wants to live with an emotionally unavailable man and his latest squeeze, who am I to question him? I've done everything I can to help him."

Javvy rose from the sofa and padded toward me, concern etched on his face, and it made me angry. I didn't need his pity.

"Come here," he murmured, reaching out for me but stubbornly, I pulled away. I can't say why I was giving him a hard time. He only meant to comfort me, after all. He wasn't my enemy.

"Hey," he said, some hurt in his voice. "I'm just trying to help, Aura."

I exhaled slowly and nodded, shooting him an apologetic look.

"I know," I sighed. "I'm sorry."

I allowed him to embrace me, relishing the feel of his well-formed chest against me. He smelled completely natural, cologne from the previous day having faded away into the pheromones of his skin, and I inhaled deeply.

His hands splayed against my back, pulling me tighter against him and almost immediately, I began to relax.

He's got the Midas touch, I thought, allowing myself to fall into him as his fingers kneaded into my back in a half-massage.

"Why don't you get out of those clothes, and I'll give you a rub down?" he offered. I wasn't going to refuse that.

"Let me jump in the shower first," I replied, pulling back slightly to kiss his full mouth. "I still smell like stale beer."

"You smell delicious," he countered. "But if you want to shower, have at it. I'll dig out the massage oils and candles."

I felt a shiver of warmth slide through me.

How did I get so lucky? He's gorgeous, he's thoughtful, and he loves me. Life does not get much better than this. Forget about everyone else; Javvy and I live in our own world. I don't give a rat's ass about anyone else.

Reluctantly, I moved toward the bathroom, teasingly stripping off my clothes as I moved.

"If you keep that up, you're not getting a massage or a shower."

"Hey," I protested. "You promised!"

"Then stop teasing me and get to it!" he growled, and I laughed, slamming the bathroom door behind me.

It took me less than ten minutes to soap myself up and wash my hair. I even managed to shave my legs in record time because the anticipation was killing me. I'd never known a man to overtake me the way Javvy had. He owned me: mind, body, and soul.

I barely toweled myself off before throwing open the door to the bathroom in a puff of steam. I didn't expect to see Javvy sitting on the sofa, and I stopped in my tracks, the smile falling from my lips as I read the expression on his face.

"Babe? What's wrong?" I demanded, my heart leaping into my throat. I rushed toward him, leaving wet footprints on the cheap linoleum, my dark hair dripping against my naked shoulders.

"Javier, what's wrong?" I demanded, falling onto the worn grey sofa at his side. "Look at me?"

He did as instructed, his face blank as he waved his cell phone at me.

"Jake..." he mumbled.

I was increasingly confused.

"Something happened to Jake?" I asked, my heart thudding against my ribs. "Is he all right?"

"Nothing happened to Jake. Jake called," he breathed, his words coming out in short pants.

"What did he say?"

Javvy wasn't making much sense, but I knew pushing him wouldn't move things along. Obviously, something bad had happened. I just needed to be patient until Javvy found the right way to say it.

"Did something happen at work?" I offered, trying to give him an out. "Was there an accident? A recall?"

Shameful as it was to admit, those things happened all the time. It was the cost of doing business, terrible as it was. Yet there was no reason for Javvy to appear so stunned unless it was a much bigger deal than usual. I was growing dizzy at the idea that people may have been injured or killed in one of the factories.

But why would Jake call Javvy about that? Javvy is head administrator, not the COO. He should be calling George.

Javvy's head whipped up, and he gaped at me. For a long moment, he didn't speak.

"Javvy?" I whispered, dread seizing me. "What is it?"

"It's Dad," he finally said. "He's dead."

CHAPTER SIX
JAVVY

I stared out the window of the office, my mind in shambles as the sunshine peaked over San Jose. The phone was ringing, but I ignored it. It never stopped anyway, even when I told the airheaded receptionist to hold my calls.

"Mr. Child, you have Barry Goldstein on line one," Amanda intoned through the intercom, but I dismissed her too. I didn't want to deal with any of it.

"Javier, you need to deal with this," Jake sighed. "I know it was all thrust on you but—"

"You deal with it!" I snapped, whirling back to stare at the VP with disgust. "He put you as his second in command. You deal with the mess he left behind!"

Jake seemed unfazed by my outburst and sat back leisurely, lifting an ankle to rest across his stupidly expensive Gucci pants.

"The company is yours now, Javier, whether or not you like it. That means that the financials are yours, too."

"Mr. Child?" Amanda called out again, and I stormed over to the phone, jabbing my finger against the comm.

"How many times do I have to tell you to hold my calls?" I roared. "HOLD. MY. CALLS. All of them!"

I heard her gasp at my biting tone, but I was far too upset to feel contrite. Amanda had never known me to raise my voice, but then again, Amanda had never known me as the CEO of Child Motors.

Goddamn you, Dad! I cursed my dead father, knowing it was wrong. *How could you leave this pile of shit for me to figure out?*

I thought the will reading had been a joke.

"No," I denied flatly when the lawyer told me, looking around the room for some support, but there was no one there but Jake who nodded serenely. Aura had offered to attend with me, but I didn't want her bored to tears by the semantics of estate law. Anyway, she had a shift that night, and she'd already called into work once to attend the funeral and viewings. I couldn't ask her to sit through this, too.

Even my mom had called, asking if she could fly down, but I sensed she was relieved my dad was dead, even though she would never say it.

I told her to stay wherever she was. I assumed she was still in San Fernando, but I didn't ask.

It had just been Jake and I in that stuffy, barely air-conditioned room, listening to the attorney explain to me that I now owned everything of my father's.

Before I could question why he had left it to me, the reasoning became clear.

"The company is in financial straits," the lawyer explained. She was a stunningly attractive woman of forty-something who wore the quintessential air of stuck-up, ivy-league attitude.

"Ah," I snorted. "Of course, it is."

It was the only reason why George would have left it to me.

"We need to speak with accounting and PR," Jake offered as I began to pace around the room. "Our investors are nervous with you in charge."

"I'm nervous with me in charge!" I roared back. "But what choice do I have?"

My gut was telling me to sell and walk away from the company once and for all, but something was holding me back. I couldn't be sure if it was some misplaced sense of loyalty or just a commonplace stubbornness that I had inherited, but I didn't want to dump Child Motors on someone else.

At least not until I've exhausted every avenue to make it right.

"You can't avoid the investors—"

"Jesus Christ, Jake, don't you think I know that? But I can't very well tell them nothing, can I? They're already on edge. Nothing I say is going to make them feel better about what's happening."

"Saying nothing isn't putting their minds at ease either, Javier."

"Can you just leave me alone for a few minutes?" I barked, knowing I was about to lose my temper. Jake eyed me warily.

"Wallowing about isn't going to solve anything, Javvy. We need to come up with a plan—"

"Jake, with all due respect, you've been VP for five minutes. You know about as much about what this company needs as the mail-room guy."

Jake sneered at me, showing a set of nicotine-stained teeth.

"And yet your father named me VP," he reminded me cruelly.

"Yeah, my father was a great man who ran a multibillion-dollar empire into debt. You must be very proud."

Jake's smirk faded, and he jumped up from the leather loveseat where he had been lounging.

"Your attitude isn't helping things," he snapped.

"You tossing around blatantly obvious statements isn't either," I reminded him. We glared at each other for a minute until he broke first, spinning to leave me alone in the office.

The phone started to ring again, and I hit the mute button, measuring my breaths in the name of calm. When the red light stopped flashing, I punched the intercom.

"Amanda, get Isobel Carlyle and Jenna Bower in here stat."

The only sensible thing which Jake had said all morning was that I needed to devise a plan with accounting and PR. We needed a budget and damage control immediately. I had no idea if I could save the company, but I was sure as hell going to do my best before I walked away from it and never looked back.

. . .

IT WAS after midnight when I walked into El Chapo. I was burnt out, but I needed to see Aura before I could even think about sleeping.

Her eyes lit up like glowing emeralds when she saw me.

"Baby!" she squealed, jumping out from behind the bar to throw her arms around me and kiss my face. Pulling back and eyeing me squarely, she said, "You look like shit."

I guffawed.

"Thanks," I replied, returning her warm embrace. I instantly felt my body relaxing as if she had some magical touch. She made the entire hellish day vanish.

"Scotch?" she asked, retreating behind the bar. "I barely heard from you all day. I was getting worried about you."

"I was in meetings," I sighed. "I meant to call you but..."

I trailed off and shook my head. She didn't need to know the sordid details of what was happening at the company. She was still an employee, even though I had told her that she didn't need to work anymore. Child Motors may be in financial ruins, but Dad had left me a pretty penny in his personal accounts. The life insurance had paid out without any issue, the aneurysm which claimed him undisputed. I was still an heir to hundreds of millions of dollars and a house which was too big for one person, no matter how many staff members milled about doing nothing.

Aura stayed at the mansion with me most nights, but she maintained her apartment, much to my annoyance. I wondered if it was because she didn't trust in our future together, but I didn't voice my insecurity aloud. It simply festered in the back of my mind, spreading slowly like a fungus.

"You look so stressed, babe," Aura told me, sliding the tumbler toward me, and I took it gratefully, swigging it back in one sip. She eyed me and reached for the glass to refill it. "That bad, huh?"

"He left me a pile of shit to deal with. I don't know if it will ever be sorted."

Aura patted my hand reassuringly.

"You've been training for this your entire life," she reminded me, passing me another drink. "Take it easy with that one; you're driving."

"Are you coming home tonight?" I asked her, and her brow furrowed slightly.

"I was planning on going to your place," she replied in confusion. "Or should I go home?"

A spark of irritation slid through me.

"I meant the mansion." I wanted her to start thinking of the estate as home.

"Oh. Well then, yes, I'm going to your place."

I lowered my gaze, my shoulders tensing, and she noticed immediately.

"Javvy, what's wrong?" she murmured. "Is this too much for you?"

I snorted at the stupidity of the question.

"Of course, it's too much for me! Dad left me in the dark, and now I'm basically running the company blind. No one respects me because they all know that. This is not a good situation."

"You can make it a good situation. Think about what you can do for your employees now!"

The excitement in her voice gave me a frisson of apprehension, but I only nodded as she continued to chirp away, oblivious to what was really happening. I was looking at mass layoffs and cutbacks at the company. I might have to close down plants and offices across the States and the UK, and she was babbling about reinstating the health insurance.

"You'll be a hero among your people!" she giggled as she leaned forward to grasp my hands. "I can't wait to tell everyone what you're going to do for them."

"Don't be dumb, Aura!"

I hadn't meant to sound so harsh or condescending, but the words were already out before I had a chance to stop them. Hurt and shock colored her expression, and she slowly stood back, removing her hands from mine.

"Pardon me?"

It was too late to backpedal now. Anyway, she needed to know what was at stake before she started shooting off her mouth, making promises that I couldn't keep.

"I'm the CEO now. I'm not one of you. I can't just jump at the employees' whims."

Her mouth pursed into a line so narrow, it almost disappeared.

"I see," she muttered, turning her head slightly so I couldn't read her expression. "So, you're just going to enforce whatever penny-pinching crap your father had going on, so you can live in your mansion?"

The ice in her tone was unmistakable, and I sucked in a breath. It was difficult to explain to her that the company and the personal finances were two completely separate issues. All I could do on my end was pay myself less, but the assets in the house had nothing to do with Child Motors.

"It's not like that, Aura," I told her, taking another swig of my drink. I was surprised to see my hands were shaking, but under the almost-murderous glare of my girlfriend, it was hard not to feel uneasy. I had handled it badly, but I was too tired to make it right. If I said anything more, I'd probably make it worse before I made it better.

"Why don't you enlighten me then?" she hissed, folding her arms under her ample chest as she glowered. "Or am I too dumb to understand?"

Yeah, it was definitely not the time to delve into this further. She was looking for a fight, and it was not the time nor place.

"I need to get to bed," I mumbled, rising from the barstool. "I'll see you when you get home."

"Your father's house is not my home," she spat. "And aren't you going to pay for your drinks? Seems like you have more than enough money now that you're taking it from your employees."

I groaned to myself and reached into my back pocket for my wallet.

"Aura, you don't know what you're talking about. We'll discuss it more when you're done work, okay?"

A sardonic smirk fell on her lips.

"Oh, I don't know," she replied in a ditzy voice, fanning herself with her hand as if she was a helpless heroine of Western romances. "I probably won't be able to keep up with your manly brain."

I clamped my mouth shut and left, knowing that we were seconds away from a blow out.

I really couldn't tell her about the money troubles at Child Motors. Ethically, it was a breach and moreover, it would worry her, not only for her own job but those of our coworkers. And she would be right to worry.

On the other hand, if I didn't explain what was going on, she would think I was on some kind of greedy power trip.

It wasn't until I got into the 2018 Powerhouse XT, my father's favorite car, that I realized why I was so irked by what had happened.

If she thinks I would purposely screw the employees to line my own pockets, she doesn't know me as well as I thought she did.

The realization stabbed me in the heart unexpectedly, and I sat back against the leather seat and stared at El Chapo's.

Could it be that maybe I didn't know Aura as well as I thought either?

CHAPTER SEVEN
AURA

I felt like he was hiding things from me, and it wasn't a good sensation. Almost overnight, we'd gone from two kids in love to being wary and suspicious of one another. If we weren't fighting, we weren't talking.

Mose nights, I spent at my own place; the cavernous walls of the mansion seemed to haunt me when I was there. Don't get me wrong; the house was gorgeous with its marble and wainscoting. I would be insane not to marvel at the beautiful artwork and calamander flooring. It truly belonged in Town and Country, but it was also alive with the memory of George Child.

It hadn't occurred to me that Javvy found peace in the house in the absence of his father. To me, it seemed that the greedy CEO's spirit had seeped into the walls like Cimmerian with unseen tentacles of darkness reaching out to claim the happy-go-lucky soul of his son.

I tried to reason that the changes were hard on Javvy, but I couldn't bear the way he spoke to me. I seemed to annoy him with my presence, and if I was being fair, his lack of desire to better our lives as employees drove me crazy. If I ever broached the subject of throwing us a bone, even a small gesture of good faith, it turned into a diatribe like I'd murdered his dog.

So, I stopped bringing it up, and the weeks dragged on with our relationship in limbo. I didn't want to end things with us. It had been so good at the beginning; it felt so right. I knew we could reclaim what we'd had if I could just get him to relax a little bit? But how? I had no way of knowing if things would ever calm down.

I sat at my desk, feeling slightly dizzy.

"Are you going to answer that?" Steph growled as she walked past my cubicle, and it was only then I realized that my phone was ringing. I had thought the noise was all in my ears.

The lack of sleep and stress was beginning to affect me daily. I was running myself too ragged, but what choice did I have? If I had once entertained the idea of moving into the mansion with Javvy, now it was no longer feasible. I had no faith that our relationship was going to last past next weekend.

Bile shot up through my throat, but I choked it back and pressed the line, speaking into my headset.

"Thank you for calling Administration. How may I direct your call?"

I sent the caller through the proper channel and then leapt to my feet, tossing the headset onto the desk.

"Aura, what the hell—?"

I was gone, shooting through the corridor toward the bathroom, and I barely made it through the door when the vomit filled my mouth. Thankfully, I made it to the toilet, spitting up and coughing.

I heard the door open, and I pushed the stall shut.

"Are you sick?" Steph demanded coldly. "You shouldn't come to work when you're sick. You'll get everyone else sick."

"I'm not sick," I snapped. "The milk in my cereal must have been bad this morning."

"Hmm," she replied, still standing outside the stall. "Maybe you should go home anyway. You're totally spaced out today. Probably from banging the boss all night."

I bristled and yanked the stall open to glare at her from my crouched position.

"I'm fine."

She shrugged.

"I have no idea why you're working at all. You scored the jackpot with Javier. Or is he making you keep working?"

Her questions were beginning to piss me off, and I rose unsteadily to my feet, unsure if I was done expelling everything which needed to come out.

"Steph, when did you and I become BFFs?" I managed, my red eyes narrowing. "Why don't you go back to work and mind your own damned business."

She eyed me with some surprise, clearly unaccustomed to me talking back, but my nerves were far too taut to mind my manners. Especially when I was being interrogated by my bitchy boss.

"Ooh," she chuckled. "Trouble in paradise."

"Steph," I said warningly. "If you don't – "

"Attention all employees!" A voice over the loudspeaker interrupted my threat. "Please report back to your desks for an important announcement. Our CEO and president, Javier Child has circulated an e-mail to everyone."

Steph and I exchanged a look.

"What's this about?" she demanded, and I shrugged my shoulders.

"How the hell do I know?"

"Well you *are* sleeping with the boss," she reminded me, and I clenched my hands into fists, willing myself not to strike her.

"You good?" she asked, watching me unsteadily walk to the sink to wash my hands. My heels felt impossibly high, and my body was aching. Maybe I was getting the flu after all.

"I don't need a babysitter," I retorted. "Go, unless you have to pee."

To my relief, she disappeared, leaving me to stare at myself in the mirror. I was pale, and my stomach was still shifting in waves of discontent, but I took a deep breath and that seemed to help—at least for the minute.

I continued to stare at myself in the mirror, trying to remember a key piece of personal information, but it wasn't coming to me easily.

No, it came last month...didn't it?

I bit on my lower lip, wracking my brain, but before I could consider the question, the door to the bathroom burst open, and half a dozen ladies walked in, their faces gaunt.

"I can't fucking believe this!" Sarah sniffled, her brown eyes filled with tears. "First our insurance, now this!"

"What a bastard. Just like his father," Jocelyn agreed, putting an arm around Sarah's shoulders, and I stared at them.

"What's going on?"

They all stopped and peered at me as if they only just realized I was standing there. Jocelyn's mouth curled into a sneer.

"Oh, but I bet you were spared, weren't you?" she asked tauntingly. "I bet you even got a raise."

"I have no idea what you're talking about. Spared from what?"

I looked at the other women, but they lowered their eyes, and the bathroom door opened again, with more upset bodies flooding inside.

"You really don't know?" Carla whispered, and I shook my head.

"Half the department got laid off. They're claiming budget cuts."

Shock hit me, and I was swooning again. I had to steady myself against the counter.

"Whatever," Jocelyn snapped. "You had to have known."

"I didn't!" I insisted, fighting through the growing crowd as claustrophobia began to settle in.

What the hell is going on? Why would he do this? Why would he do this without telling me?

I made my way to my desk and saw Steph shaking her head as she stared at me. I was the enemy suddenly even though I'd had no part of anything going on.

My cell phone was ringing and without glancing at it, I knew it was Javvy, but I didn't bother answering it. I had to check my work e-mail to see what fate had in store for me.

Beads of sweat broke out over my face, and I sank into my chair as my fingers worked furiously over the computer.

The e-mail was there, although I don't know why I was shocked to see it.

Dear Valued Employee,

Due to recent budget cuts, we regret to inform you that effective immediately, the following employees will be laid off from their positions at Child Motors until further notice. Please be assured we are doing all we can to reinstate these jobs at our earliest convenience.

Thank you for your dedicated service to our company and we look forward to working with you again.

Javier Child

President and CEO

As I continued to scroll, I read that what Jocelyn had said was true: half the department had been let go.

And my name was on the list.

Indignation, disgust, and fury flooded me like a tsunami of sick. I couldn't see; my eyes were red and hazy.

"Real trouble in paradise, huh?" Steph snickered, and I reached for the closest thing on my desk which I promptly whipped at her head. Thankfully—or maybe not—it was an unsharpened pencil and not a stapler.

I rose to my feet and grabbed my purse, stumbling from the office. I could hear my phone ringing again where I'd left it, but I wasn't going back for it. I wouldn't be able to afford it in a few weeks anyway.

How could he do this to us? Why didn't he at least warn me?

I knew he'd have some explanation for what he'd done, but I didn't want to hear it. This was just confirmation of what I'd already known. I'd been trying to ignore the signs, but it was impossible to do that now, not when he was purposely slapping me in the face with it.

Javier Child was becoming his father, whether I liked it or not, and there was nothing I could do or say to change it.

Even if I go and scream in his face, it won't change anything. He's lost the respect of the employees, and he's certainly lost mine.

A part of me wondered if this wasn't some sick way of forcing me to move in with him, by taking away my livelihood. I still had El Chapo but that wasn't going to sustain me.

I forsook the elevator and bolted down the stairs, the confused echoes of the staff still ringing in my ears as I moved.

I'll figure out a way to survive, I thought tensely. *I always have.*

I didn't need to beg Javier for help. I'd obviously made a mistake; I'd picked the wrong guy, but women had made worse mistakes than that.

No, I was done. I would forget about him, no matter how upset I was in that moment, no matter how hard it was to believe he'd done something so callous.

Money makes people do awful things. I don't need to hear his excuses. The bottom line is that he did something which is inexcusable.

I was panting when I reached the lobby, but I ducked into the parking lot and fumbled for my keys, eager to put as much distance between me and the building as humanly possible.

I was overcome by another sweep of dizziness as I collapsed into the hot car, and I waited it out for a minute, feeling the bubble of nausea sweep through me.

Other employees began to filter out the doors, casting me odd looks as they passed, and I knew I was probably deathly pale, but I barely noticed them. My mind was elsewhere as the question resurfaced in a bolt of lightning.

When was the last time I got my period?

Yet no matter how long I sat, sweating in my overheated car, I could not recall the answer.

CHAPTER EIGHT

JAVVY

Two Years Later

"The car is waiting for you, Mr. Child," Cory announced from the open doorway of my suite.

"I'll be down in a minute," I sighed, eyeing my reflection in the mirror critically. How long had it been since I'd been to a wedding, any wedding?

It wasn't really my scene, and the idea of romance was not anything I would consider celebratory, not since losing Aura so abruptly years before.

I frowned, furious that I was letting her creep into my thoughts again after all that time, even though I'd vowed not to let anything ruin the day.

I forced myself to give myself one last once-over. I looked great if I did say so myself. My dark blonde hair swept back from my face, showing off my regal cheekbones handsomely. My tux was a custom fit, the usual penguin style, double breasted and deep ebony. It was only an hour and a half to the venue via jet, but I'd put on my cummerbund after I arrived.

I spun from the glass and reached for my wallet to meet the car.

My mother was getting remarried after being alone for thirteen years. The least I could do was be there for her, even though I'd only seen her once since my father had died.

I had yet to meet my future stepfather nor my stepsiblings, but if I was being honest, I didn't really care. Those people were strangers to me, not family, and while I would be there for my mother, I knew I'd probably never see her husband again.

"Cory, you sent the check to the house already, yes?" I asked my assistant, and he nodded.

"Yes, sir. They should have it already."

I nodded. I had sent a sizeable fortune in the way of a wedding present because what did I know about picking out gravy boats? Anyway, if I knew anything about my mom, she would find the cash more useful than any fine china. I didn't know much about Mitch Harper, the man she was marrying, but from what I'd gleaned, he was of a humble background.

It didn't matter; I had the money to give. In eighteen months, I had managed to bring Child Motors up from drowning in the red to showing a tidy profit. It had taken more cuts and negotiating than I would have liked, but the car company was finally back to what it once was: a symbol of prestige and luxury.

I slipped into the limo and sat back against the coolness of the seat, closing my eyes. I was so tired. A part of me wished I'd arranged for the five-and-a-half-hour car trip, if only to catch up on some sleep, but there were just not enough hours in the day. I'd been working from dawn already.

"We'll be at the airfield in fifteen minutes," the driver announced, and I nodded.

Fifteen minutes was more than enough time to nap.

～

THE SUN WAS scorching through the back of my tux as I stepped from the taxi, but I barely noticed it as I looked around the festive villa. It was something straight out of a Mexican fairy tale and I had to grin at the almost obnoxiously bright colors.

Do Mexicans even get married like this or is this just expats bastardizing their traditions?

I had to admit that it was beautiful, strings of lights interlacing around the entire framework of the house, colorful piñatas and flowers decorating every surface I could see.

As I approached the arched entryway, the structure reminiscent of the Alamo, I heard someone calling to me in Spanish.

"Javier! *Venga, mijo!*"

I turned, recognizing my mother's voice instantly, and my heart warmed as I caught a glimpse of her in an off-the-shoulder white dress of sheer lace. Her raven hair fell over her olive shoulders as she smiled at me, her brilliant white teeth a sharp contrast to that tanned flesh.

Her blue eyes studied my face curiously.

"I can't believe you're here!" she gasped, hurrying to sweep me into an embrace. I laughed nervously, but I didn't pull away, inhaling her floral perfume. She had barely aged a day since childhood.

"Of course I came! You're getting married!"

She stepped back and looked at me again as if trying to gauge if I was happy or miserable.

"You look beautiful, but isn't the bride supposed to stay hidden before the ceremony?"

She snickered, looping her arm through mine and leading me into the courtyard.

"We're old, *mijo*," she teased. "We've given up on superstition a long time ago."

"Where is Mitch?" I asked, looking around at the ever-growing crowds to get a handle on my stepfather.

"Patience, *guapo*," she laughed. "Where do you think I'm taking you?"

"*Abuela*, can you take Ava for a minute?" A girl squeaked from behind me, and I turned to see a toddler running away from her caretaker. "I need to find her mother, but she's disappeared again!"

"*Si, amor*," my mother laughed. "Go find her and I'll watch her."

"*Abuela*?" I choked. "You're a grandmother?"

"Stepgrandmother, I suppose, but the poor child has no other grandmother. She belongs to your stepsister."

"Oh."

I realized that my mom was the referencing the baby, not the teenaged girl who ran off in a blind panic.

"Cute kid."

I found myself staring after her. She reminded me of Aura with those big green eyes and mop of dark hair, but before I could give any more thought to the newly waddling baby, a man appeared at my side, and I saw where the child got her looks from. Mitch Harper's genes ran strong. So strong, they made my heart flutter with nervousness as I stared at him.

He looks more like Aura than the kid does.

"You must be Javier. I've seen your face all over the internet in the last two years!"

"Mitch, I assume?" I replied, extending my hand to shake his hand. "I'm sorry I haven't been down here to meet you sooner."

He laughed.

"Don't worry about it. I've heard you have had your hands full. And, I'm sorry about the loss of your father."

I shot my mom a look, and she lowered her gaze.

"Thank you," I said quickly. "It was sudden."

I don't know why I added that. It was a given.

"Enough depressing talk," Mom said. "Let me find your stepsiblings. I am hoping that you will all make a toast at the reception."

"Oh, Cate, he must be exhausted. Give the boy a drink at least before shuffling him around," Mitch laughed.

"Cate?" I snickered. I'd never heard her called that before. Her name was Cateyana.

"It's Mitch's nickname for me, and it stuck around here," my mom explained, casting me a warning look as if she was worried that I would say something to embarrass her.

"Well, it's very Westernized," I teased, winking to show I was only jesting with her.

She seemed relieved, but as she looked past me, her eyes widened.

"Alex!" she called. "Alex, venga! Come and meet your stepbrother!"

My breath caught in my throat.

Alex. That is Aura's brother's name.

I shook my head at the ridiculous thought and turned to address the man stalking toward me. He, too, bore the same thick, dark hair and blazing green eyes of his family.

"Wow, Javier Child," Alex cried, grabbing my hand and pumping it vigorously. "How great to meet you. I'm Alex. Alex Cameron. Your soon-to-be brother."

The smile froze on my face as I looked around in slow motion, wondering if there were hidden cameras watching me.

Was this a joke?

"Cameron?" I repeated, my voice hoarse. "You're..."

Alex blinked at me, waiting for me to finish my sentence but I couldn't. It was surreal. They didn't share the same last name as their father.

I thought of Aura's childhood, her gambling, verbally abusive mother. She had never claimed that her parents were divorced. They could very well have been a common law couple.

I spun to my mom, my mouth parting.

"Aura."

Mom nodded agreeably.

"She's around here somewhere." She looked around, but the number of people seemed to have doubled since my arrival.

I stared at her in disbelief, wracking my brain to recall if she had ever told me the names of my stepsiblings-to-be, but I couldn't reconcile such a thing. Obviously, I would have remembered that my former lover was about to be my stepsister.

Had Aura known? If so, why hadn't she told me? Warned me?

I knew the answer; she was still furious with me. She still didn't understand why I had done what I'd done, why it had been necessary not only to make those cutbacks, but to lay her off, too.

Of course, if I'd had any inkling that she would disappear without a trace, without so much as a goodbye, I would have reconsidered my actions back then. In a million years, I had never anticipated that she would ghost me.

It had left me furious, and while I had made some half-hearted attempts to find her through social media and Google, I was far too hurt to hire an investigator to search for her. I reasoned that if she wanted to be found, she would resurface. But if she didn't want to talk to me like an adult, she could go.

It didn't change the fact that I was pained by how things had gone down, and that I had hoped for so much more from her.

"Ah, there she is!" Mitch cried, pointing, and again, time seemed to slow down.

I pivoted and indeed, there was Aura, standing not ten feet away, talking to a woman in a bright pink sundress.

She was wearing a sundress of her own, but much more elegant, cut low to show off her full bust and swelling cleavage. The off-white of the material matched my mother's dress, and I was surprised to see they were both in the same color, but that was truly the least of my concerns at that moment.

She hadn't seen me yet, but as I continued to stare at her, Mitch yelled out for her.

"Aura! Come meet your stepbrother!"

Her head jerked up, and I saw her lips tighten, but there was no surprise on her face as she excused herself from her friend and made her way over to us.

She had known!

I felt my mouth tighten to match hers in a silent scowl, and tension built in my shoulders as she drew closer, but I couldn't deny the attraction I still felt toward her. She had grown more beautiful in the past two years, her color rosy, her eyes glowing brighter than I'd ever seen them. She was radiant.

I found myself wondering if she was there with anyone.

"Aura, this is—"

"I know who he is," Aura interjected. "I used to work at his company before he laid me off."

There it was, out in the open, in front of the family.

"Aura, there was a lot happening—"

"It's ancient history," she cut in shortly, her eyes scanning the area around us. "Where's Ava?"

A strange knot formed in my stomach, and I couldn't understand why at first. It wasn't until her eyes fell on the stumbling toddler a few feet away that it all registered with a stunning blow to my gut.

"Mama!" the baby cooed, her eyes brightening as she made her way toward Aura. I watched my ex-girlfriend lean down to scoop up the baby, cuddling her close as she cast me a warning look which spoke volumes.

"Well," Alex chuckled. "This is awkward."

"No, it's not!" my mom insisted, also giving me a scathing look. I was beginning to feel like I did in my father's presence, reprimanded and small but it was nothing compared to the anger that was brewing in me as I stared at Ava, searching for any semblance of me in her.

How old was the child? Could she be mine?

"Okay, Mitchie. Time to get married, honey," Mom chirped, and he nodded in agreement, winking at us.

"It's the moment I've been waiting for," he agreed, taking his fiancée's arm. "We'll see you kids after we're married."

There as nothing I could do but watch them disappear before turning back to gape at Aura.

"What?" she hissed. "Stop staring at me!"

Alex eyed us with surprise, but he shot me a grin.

"Don't take it personally," he said. "She can hold a decent grudge."

"Aura, can I talk to you for a second?" I asked from between clenched teeth, but she shook her dark waves that were pinned up with pearl combs.

"Nope. Didn't you hear? We've got a wedding to attend."

CHAPTER NINE
AURA

I learned about Javvy becoming my stepbrother a year before the wedding, and it had been a year of long, torturous journey of soul-searching for me.

I had assumed he knew, too, and had not bothered to warn me about it, waiting to see the look on my face as some kind of petty revenge, but it became obvious immediately that he knew nothing about our impending relationship when I saw him.

The truth was, I was just not ready to tell him about our baby. I knew one day I would have to come clean but there were so many factors holding me back, so many reasons not to fire him an e-mail which read, "By the way, you're a dad."

It would have been fitting to break it to him that way. After all, that was the way he'd canned me without even the decency to tell me to my face.

"Mama!" Ava cooed, yanking on my hair gently, and I smiled at her.

The service was happening, mostly in Spanish which was odd because I doubt there were even a dozen Spanish-speaking guests in the villa but it was beautiful all the same. I was happy for my dad, and I really liked Cate. She reminded me of what Javvy was like before he turned into a greedy tyrant like his father.

I had packed up my meager belongings the very day I'd been laid off and gone to the pharmacy for a pregnancy test.

It only confirmed what I already knew, and from there, I had to make some decisions with my life.

The first one was getting out of town.

I swallowed my pride and called Alex who had been inordinately pleased when I told him I wanted to move in with him and Dad in Tijuana. I was sure Dad would have a fit, but to my shock, he welcomed me with open arms.

"Cate's mellowed him out," Alex explained. "She's got the patience of a saint, I swear. I don't know how she puts up with him."

They didn't question me about the father of the baby until after Ava was born, and by then, I had learned that Javvy was Cate's son.

What kind of fate-driven hell am I living in? I wondered, shaking my head as I thought about the chances of that happening. What were the odds? One in millions? Billions?

It didn't matter anyway. Javvy and I weren't going to be together, but how weird was it going to be for my dad and Cate to learn that their granddaughter was doubly a granddaughter.

Very Appalachian, I mused dryly, but even as I thought about it, I realized that Dad had been with Cate first, or very close to the same time as Javvy and I had gotten together. I never really asked for specific dates because honestly, I didn't want to know.

So, I knew Javvy was coming, and that he'd put two and two together to see that the little girl was likely his child. It had occurred to me to lie and tell him that she was younger or older, but I'd had enough dancing around the issue. He knew, or at least he should have known, and we'd have to decide together what to tell our parents.

It filled me with an unbearable sick feeling, wondering how they would react when they found out. They had both been incredible, letting me stay at their picturesque hacienda while encouraging me to finish the novel I'd been working on since my teens.

After I'd done that, Cate hooked me up with a publisher she knew and got me started with a marketing campaign, making the book a bestseller in six weeks. The royalties weren't millions of dollars, but they were sustaining me enough to get me working on the second book in the series. I was on a creative roll that would never have happened if they hadn't taken me in.

"You have the hots for your stepbrother."

Alex's voice shot me back to reality, and I eyed him with contempt.

"Shut up!" I snapped under my breath. "You're disgusting."

"I'm not the one staring at him like a lost puppy," he replied, laughing, and I punched him in the arm. "Did you guys have a thing back in San Jose?"

"Alex, our father is getting married. Show a little respect!"

He shrugged but I could feel him leering at me as I tried to watch the ceremony with Ava climbing all over me.

But my brother was right; I couldn't keep my eyes off my former lover.

At the pulpit, the minister intoned something else, and Dad slipped a ring onto Cate's finger as he gazed lovingly into her eyes.

He's not your former lover anymore. Now he's family.

I TRIED my best to avoid Javvy, but I knew he would inevitably catch up with me. I paced around one of the guest bedrooms, staring out into the pool area. The glass was tinted so no one could see inside, but I had a clear view of all the well-wishers milling about, drinking champagne and toasting the newlyweds.

Javvy must have been looking for me, and that was where he found me, sitting on the gleaming hardwood, my back against the bed piled up with coats as I tried to think of my next move.

"You can't expect to hide here forever," he snarled, stalking toward me, and I jumped to my feet in alarm, not liking the anger in his face.

"I'm not hiding. I'm just...escaping the crowds for a bit," I replied lamely. I could see he wasn't buying it in the least.

He stepped towards me until our faces were inches from each

other, and I jutted my chin out defiantly as I silently dared him to be angry. He had no right to barge in, all full of piss and vinegar. He was the one who had screwed everything up. This was not my fault.

"Is she mine?"

Well, there was that...he did have a right to be mad about Ava. For a fleeting moment, I considered lying, but I couldn't do it. I'd already kept him away from her for a year.

What was wrong with me to do that? I had always resented my own mother for keeping us from Mitch, but he hadn't wanted us either. I had always vowed that when I had children, they would know their father, even if he and I weren't together.

"Yes," I mumbled. "She is."

He choked and paled, stepping back as if the confirmation had stabbed him.

"Wh— How could you not tell me, Aura? Wh— How? Why?"

The anguish in his voice pierced my heart, and I was flooded with shame as I dropped my head.

"Because..." I sighed. "Because I thought it was the best thing for Ava at the time, but by the time I changed my mind, it was too late, knowing that our parents were getting married. I didn't want this to ruin anything for them. I was going to tell you—"

"HOW CAN KEEPING A CHILD FROM HER FATHER BE GOOD?" He screamed, his face flushing with fury, and I inhaled sharply, slightly afraid as he advanced on me. But more than scared, I was suddenly aroused, forgetting the power he had over me. He had always made me weak in the knees and seeing him like that, so riled up, so...dangerous—well, it turned me on.

And I wasn't ashamed in the least.

"You were acting like your father," I answered simply. "I wouldn't think you would have wanted your child to be raised the same way you were."

He froze where he stood, a look of uncertainty flooding his face as my words hit home. It had never dawned on him until that moment that maybe my actions weren't spiteful.

"I'm not my father," he mumbled, the fire in his eyes diminishing, but he was still angry enough to keep my pulse racing. "I would never do anything to hurt our child."

"I don't think you would intentionally hurt her," I conceded quickly, reaching down to touch his arm. I felt the electricity I knew so well bolt between us, and I sighed, knowing I wanted to feel him inside me, if only once more.

His eyes traveled up to my face, and our eyes locked, the emotion that coursed between us unmistakable. He had missed me as much as I had him.

I lowered myself beside him, reaching up to cup his face between my palms. My heart was thudding so intently, I was sure he could hear it, but if he couldn't, there was no way he could miss it pulsing along my fingertips.

"I missed you," he told me, and the sincerity rang so true, it made me fill with melancholy.

Instead of answering, I pressed my lips to his, softly but firmly, drawing him close. My lids dropped; I could still read the expression on his face, but I was already floating out of my body as I tended to do within his embrace.

Gently, he pushed me back against the pile of shawls and light jackets littering the bed top, his mouth curving over the line of my chin as his hand scooped under me to raise my ass upward.

I sighed deeply, knowing that I had been pining for this moment for two years, even though I never really believed that Javvy would still want me the way I had always wanted him. Even in my anger, I'd longed to catch a glimpse of his face, however briefly at the bodega or on the dusty, crowded Tijuana streets. I wrote about him in my novel, trying to bring the power of our connection to the pages, but I was sure I hadn't done it any justice. How could I? It was impossible to put such a feeling to words.

His lips worked across my clavicles, missing nothing as he breathed me in, and I was melting into a puddle of desire as I yearned for him to be inside me, to consume me entirely.

"I missed you, too," I mumbled. I needed him to know that I had not forgotten about him, not for a minute.

My hips were exposed as the lace of my dress rose higher, the cool leather of someone's coat brushing against the skin of my rear.

The sensation of chill against my burning skin sent a gush through the center of my being, and Javvy's hands moved down to explore the dampness in between as his fingers spread me apart.

"God, you're always so wet!"

"Only for you," I heard myself say, but my mind was somewhere else, all my awareness focused solely on his touch, my body quivering in response.

Lower his head dropped, seeking out my hottest spot, his lips latching around my drenched lips, and I cried out, my nub swollen and throbbing. His tongue circled me slowly but firmly, moving exactly the way he knew I liked it.

He hasn't forgotten, I thought, the realization driving me higher. I'd been such a fool to walk away from him, no matter how mad I'd been. He and I belonged together; it was obvious in the way we fit together.

Harder his tongue moved now, sensing my body preparing to explode, and moans escaped my mouth in rapid succession until I couldn't bear anymore. I released against his mouth, feeling him lap every drop of my climax as I bucked, dangerously close to catching his teeth against my burning clit.

I barely had time to fully release when suddenly I was face first in the pile of coats, my cheeks spread wide behind me.

I gasped, remembering how big he was, never more so than when he took me like that.

I was about to call out for him to go slow, but he was already inside me, my muscles contracting around his enormous shaft as if to swallow him fully.

"Fuck!" I mewled, feeling him deep, but he had no intention of slowing down, that much was clear. It was as if he was pouring all the anger he felt into rocking my body as he drove me relentlessly into the soft pile under me.

My breath caught in my throat, and I was unable to cry out, but it hurt so good.

"I'd almost forgotten how tight you are," he grunted breathlessly, and on cue, I clasped the muscles of my core around him. A loud, defeated moan fell from his mouth, and he spilled inside me in scalding streaks of lava.

I was immobilized as his seed filled me, but I continued to constrict myself around his pulsating member until I was sure I'd coaxed every drop from him.

He fell on top of me in an unceremonious heap, his mouth against my earlobe. The feel of his breath against my ear sent shivers up and down my spine.

"You have a thing for coats," he commented dryly, lifting himself up off my back a moment later, and I turned to peer at him.

"I think I have a thing for you," I replied quietly.

CHAPTER TEN
JAVVY

We straightened ourselves out, sitting back up on the bed. "What are we going to do about this, Javvy?" Aura asked me, and I cast her a sidelong look.

"What's the issue?"

She snorted, her eyes narrowing as if she thought I was mocking her, but I genuinely didn't see the problem.

"The issue is, we're related now," she reminded me, and I cringed slightly at the idea.

"Not by blood," I snapped. "And don't say that. It creeps me out."

"Well, imagine what's going to happen when Ava gets older, and people tell her that her parents are stepsiblings. Something like this can and will ruin your business."

I stared at her in shock, my brow furrowing.

"You think I give a shit about the business?" I almost laughed. "Christ, you really don't know me at all, do you?"

"I know that you had no problem firing a bunch of us while you hid behind an e-mail," she shot back, and I knew I deserved that, but I remained defensive.

"It wasn't like that, Aura. I had no choice but to make cutbacks.

My dad left me with a legacy that was bankrupt. I had to make decisions, hard decisions."

Her face twisted, and she gaped at me.

"Why didn't you tell me that?" she choked. "I could have helped you if I'd known."

"How?" I asked. "How were you going to get us half a billion dollars out of debt? I had to work for free for eighteen months and cut everything. We were balancing on a tightrope, but I made it out. I hired almost everyone back, Aura. I'm almost back to where we started."

Her jaw went slack, and I could see she was stunned.

"I couldn't tell you. It was unethical. You were an employee, and there was always a chance you could tell someone and raise alarm."

"I would never!"

"You probably wouldn't, Aura, but I was in a tight spot. It wasn't that I didn't trust you, but this was a work situation, one that had nothing to do with you. I didn't even see the list of layoffs, although in hindsight, I should have known you would have been on it. I was doing my best in an impossible situation."

She didn't speak for a long moment, but I could tell she was processing the information she'd been given.

"I've always loved you, Aura. How I feel about you has never changed, and it never will, I swear. Even when I'm furious at you, I love you and can't help myself."

She offered me a smile, but I could see she was still worried.

"That doesn't change the fact that we are stepsiblings now. It doesn't matter how much we love one another, Javvy. Our relationship is going to be frowned upon, and moreover, Ava is going to suffer because of it."

She had a very valid point, and I didn't have an easy answer for any of it. All I knew was that somehow, some way, we were going to make it work and live as a family, no matter what.

. . .

AFTER THE WEDDING, I brought Aura and Ava back to San Jose with me. She was such a beautiful child, so sweet and vibrant and full of life. I was stunned by her resemblance to her mother, and I hoped that she would grow up to be as fearless as Aura.

"Alex knows something's up," Aura murmured as we reached the wrought-iron gates surrounding the property. She had been unusually quiet the entire trip back, but I didn't want to push her as to the reason why.

I already had a good idea of what was on her mind.

Ava had fallen asleep in that brand-new car seat that I'd asked the driver to pick up in advance.

"We were going to tell them after Mom and Mitch came home," I reminded her. "Anyway, he doesn't seem like he cares. He looks happy to have the villa to himself."

She didn't smile, and I felt a pang of worry as the town car pulled up outside the Tudor-style doors.

"What are we doing, Javvy?" she muttered. "We can't do this. This is Ava's future at stake—and your business."

"Yes," I commented dryly. "These are points you have already offered, and I thought we decided that we'll figure something out, right?"

"We have to figure something out first and then be together," she blurted out nervously as the driver opened her side of the vehicle. "Before anyone can see us together and rumors gets started. If anyone gets a whiff of this, Javvy, we'll never get out from under it."

My eyes narrowed, and neither of us made a move to exit the car as I considered her words.

"First of all, you're not going anywhere," I told her flatly. "I have missed out on a year with my daughter and your pregnancy. If you think for a second I'm letting either one of you out of my sight, you've got another thing coming."

Our gazed locked, and we stared at each other. I knew what she was saying was true—every word of it—but I also knew there was no way I was letting her go, even for a few days.

Ava stirred in her car seat, and Aura reached for her, but I stopped her.

"Let me," I pleaded, and she immediately sat back, a look of appreciation on her face as Ava blinked her bright green eyes awake.

"Hi, baby girl," I murmured at her sweetly. "Come to Daddy."

She parted her lips uncertainly, looking from me to her mother and for a devastating second, I thought she was going to release a howl for the neighbors to hear. My breath caught in my throat as I continued to smile reassuringly at her, unbuckling the straps of the car seat before gently lifting her from the bucket.

Please don't cry, I begged her silently as if her tears would make or break Aura's decision to stay. *Look at me. I'm your Daddy.*

As if she could read my thoughts, her emerald eyes grew wider and a half-smile formed on her tiny mouth. She babbled something incoherent, raising a fist, and I released a long, shaking laugh. I don't think my heart had ever been as filled as it was in that moment.

I couldn't tear my eyes away from her precious little face, and I knew in that moment that there was nothing that I wouldn't do for that little creature. I was smitten, like I had been waiting my entire life to meet this innocent being. I also knew I would do anything and everything in my power to protect her at all cost.

"Javvy, the driver is waiting for us," Aura reminded me gently, but I didn't care. I couldn't tear my eyes away from the sweetly smiling kid with her mother's mischievous eyes.

And then, I knew what we had to do.

"Javvy..."

"I'm selling Child Motors."

The sentence came out in a rush, and she looked at me in shock.

"What? No, you can't!" Aura protested. "It's the company you saved from bankruptcy! Why would you do that?"

"It's not my company," I replied evenly. "It was my father's, and if I'm honest with myself, I never really wanted it in the first place. I think the ideal appealed to me when I was a kid. I mean what kid wouldn't want to be a billionaire some day but really, I never did."

Aura studied my face pensively.

"What would you do?" she asked quietly. "Just sit around on the beach and drink mojitos?"

I smiled, turning my attention back to Ava who snatched my finger defiantly and squeezed.

"As much as I'd love to spend every waking moment with you and this little beauty, I think I'd go crazy not being able to work. I'd just reinvest the money into another business."

"Like what?" she asked curiously.

"I have some ideas," I replied vaguely, but I didn't elaborate. I knew exactly what I was going to do and how we were going to keep our family together.

"Javier, it doesn't change anything. People will still know—"

"Do you trust me, Aura?"

The question seemed to confuse her, and I watched as she carefully considered it.

"Yes," she replied finally. "I really do. I always have, even when we never knew one another."

"Then I'm asking you to really trust me on this," I told her earnestly, and Aura nodded slowly.

"All right," she agreed softly, casting a look toward Ava who giggled at us both.

I leaned in and dropped a soft kiss on her lips.

"Give me two weeks, and we'll be living the life we always dreamed of—together."

THE END.